Meet My
FAMOUS
Friends

by Rich DiSilvio

Hardcover ISBN-13: 978-0-9976807-5-1
Paperback ISBN-13: 978-0-9976807-6-8
eBook ISBN-13: 978-0-9976807-7-5

SUBJECT CATEGORIES: Illustrious people, Famous people, Wit and humor, YA Humor, Picture books for children

Photos and images utilized from author's private collection, other images courtesy of Library of Congress public domain images and Wikipedia's public domain and Creative Commons images: Big Boy locomotive-RFM57, David-Jörg Bittner Unna, wind tunnel-Georgepehli, Victrola-Alessandro Nassiri, stein-Jaypee, record disc-Mediatus, US Capitol building, Martin Falbisoner.

The Author/Artist

Rich DiSilvio is the author of YA books, adult thrillers, mysteries, historical fiction and nonfiction. As an artist, Rich has designed numerous advertisements, book covers, and CD/DVD packages for noted authors like Clark Ashton Smith, and musical legends like Pink Floyd, Yes, Moody Blues, Rolling Stones, Black Sabbath, Elton John, Queen, Alice Cooper, Jay-Z, Willie Nelson and more.

In the entertainment field, DiSilvio has provided creative assets for films, cable TV shows, and documentaries, such as James Cameron's *The Lost Tomb of Jesus, Operation Valkyrie, Celebrity Mole, Monty Python: Almost the Truth, Tracey Ullman's State of the Union, The Man Show* etc.

Rich lives in New York with his wife, and has four children.

Website: www.richdisilvio.com

CONTENTS

The contents in this book are...well, quite bizarre! There's no need for a *Table* of Contents, since there isn't any food that I can offer you, so what good is a table anyhow?

No, no, the contents here are not eatable, but they are delectable. Figuratively speaking of course. Also, please note that this is a *picture book* with *brief captions*, so don't expect lengthy biographies! This is meant to be an appetizer to incite interest, not a full seven-course meal.

Oh dear, there I go again about food. My apologies! As I said, I'm not actually serving any food, so please put your forks, spoons, and appetites away.

Please proceed at your own risk, and keep an open mind. I take no responsibility for any confusion, insights, inspiration, perspiration, elation, or laughter you may incur. So all I can say is, "Be adventurous!"

-- Rich DiSilvio

ALL ABOARD

The journey begins with the inimitable Mark Train. What better way to start this journey than with the witty wordsmith himself.

As you continue through this visual feast...wait! Scratch that. I did say I was not offering you any food in the Contents, and I don't wish to mislead you. So, again, I state: There is no food or feast in this book, just imaginative eye candy. Oops! There I go again. It's actually quite hard to avoid mentioning food while describing this journey. Let me start again.

Okay. Mark Train begins this fascinating journey of introducing you to My Famous Friends. Although I have many other famous friends that didn't make it into this book, all of these special friends have made great contributions to mankind in one form or another, and I at least managed to fit some of them within this edition.

So despite their whimsical appearances or peculiar settings, do realize that beyond the smiles and laughter they may arouse are luminous souls that have indeed offered Western civilization enormous contributions that deserve our attention. So if adding a little humor to the mix to get people to stop in their tracks (how do you like the reference to train *tracks*?) to contemplate these people, then I'm hoping that's a noble goal.

Additionally, as Einstein said, "Imagination is more important than knowledge." Meanwhile, Steve Jobs asked us to *think differently* and indeed we must. Nothing new and inventive can materialize without the human imagination, and this book celebrates that.

Well, it looks like Mark's train is steaming along, so time to hop aboard and move on down the line. *Enjoy the ride, and let your imagination loose!*

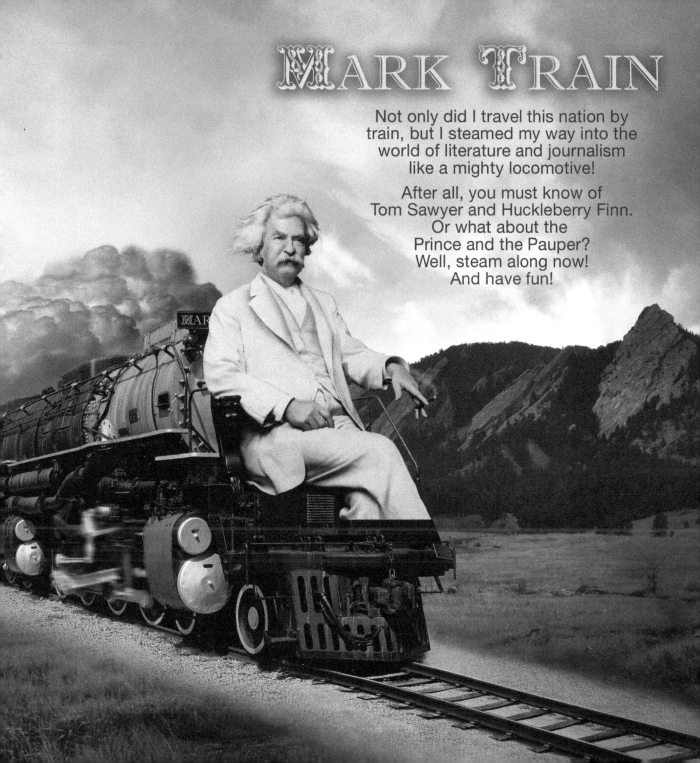

MARK TRAIN

Not only did I travel this nation by
train, but I steamed my way into the
world of literature and journalism
like a mighty locomotive!

After all, you must know of
Tom Sawyer and Huckleberry Finn.
Or what about the
Prince and the Pauper?
Well, steam along now!
And have fun!

Lionardo da Vinci

Although my mighty roar has been primarily as a painter, I also did many other things.

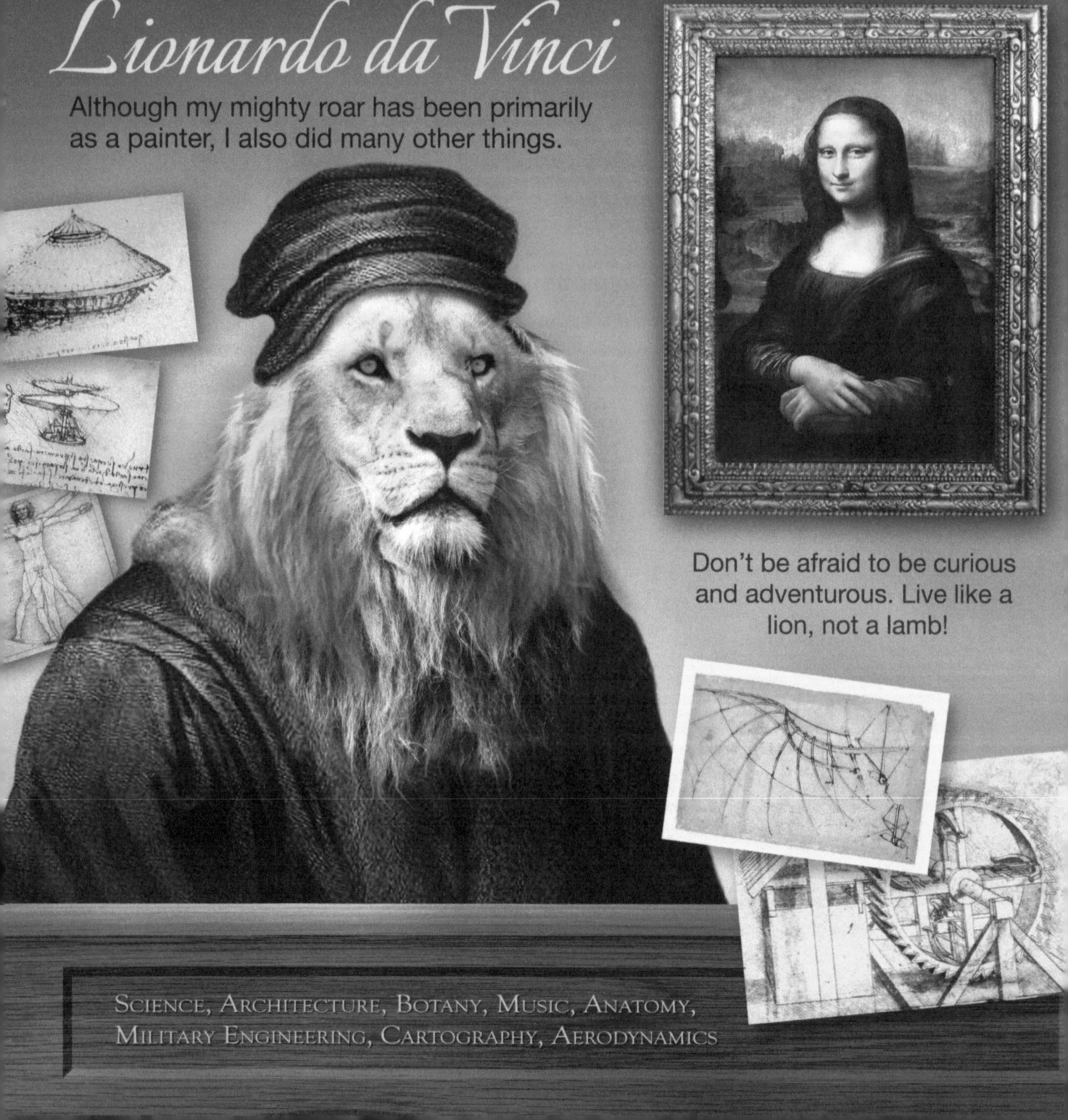

Don’t be afraid to be curious and adventurous. Live like a lion, not a lamb!

SCIENCE, ARCHITECTURE, BOTANY, MUSIC, ANATOMY, MILITARY ENGINEERING, CARTOGRAPHY, AERODYNAMICS

Amelia Airheart

Hi there! I was the first female pilot to fly solo across the Atlantic Ocean. I loved to fly high in the sky. Wanna try?

But be sure to bring a compass!

Giacomo
Poochini

Welcome to my stage.
I mean page!

I composed beautiful
music for Italian operas.
In fact, so beautiful, that
some people even
cried. Yes, it's true!
Many still do.

But even though
some sopranos can
be *ruff* on the ears,
the Pooch's operas
have lasted all
these years.

So despite all the
tears, I love all
the cheers!

Vincent van Goat

Hi, I liked to paint with colorful, long dashes. Some people think that's *baah-d*. But I hope *you* like it? What? I can't hear you. I seemed to have lost an ear!

George
WashingMachine

I hereby present to you, good citizens of the United States of America, that as a general, I washed the colonies clean of the British Redcoats!

Washing loads limited to **one ton**, or a Washing*ton*!

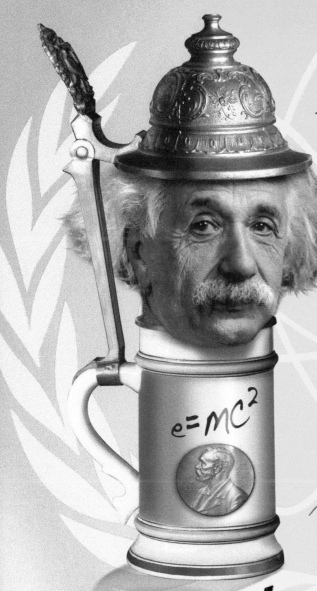

Albert
EINE-STEIN

I received world acclaim for my cryptic theory of relativity, which was relatively easy to comprehend, if you happen to be a genius. But I won the Nobel Prize for my photoelectric effect instead.

So, let's drink to *imagination*, because I believe it's more important than knowledge.

Prost! That's "Cheers" in German.

Albert Einstein

$e=mc^2$

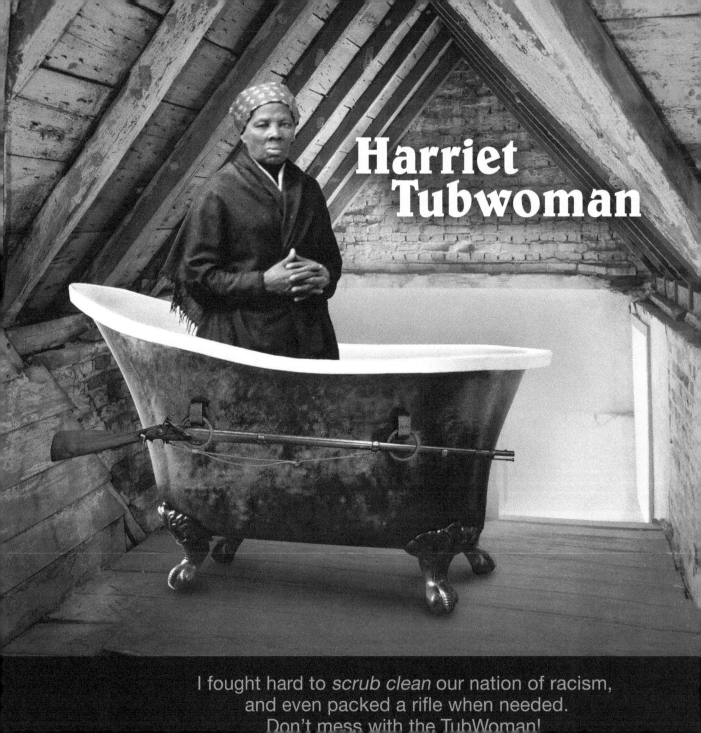

Harriet Tubwoman

I fought hard to *scrub clean* our nation of racism, and even packed a rifle when needed. Don't mess with the TubWoman!

Carrotvaggio

I loved to paint figures in **light** and darkness.
Oh, yes, and fruits & veggies, too!
Especially carrots, because they're good for your eyes!

Franz List

The List

1. I was called the *King of the Piano.*

2. I invented the piano recital and the practice of performing from memory.

3. I invented the master class.

4. I invented the symphonic poem.

5. I was a leader of the Romantic movement but also invented two new genres, impressionist and atonal.

I guess you can say, I was very... *inventive!*

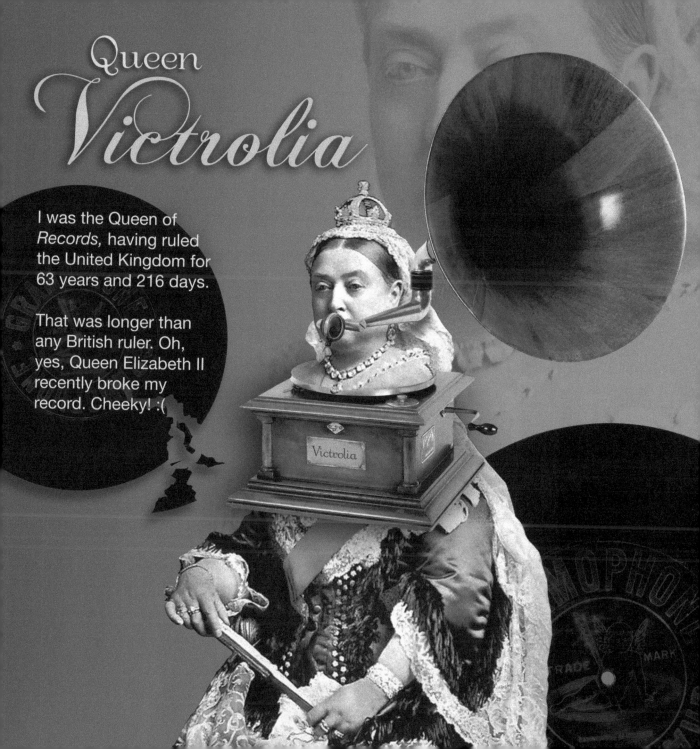

Queen *Victrolia*

I was the Queen of *Records,* having ruled the United Kingdom for 63 years and 216 days.

That was longer than any British ruler. Oh, yes, Queen Elizabeth II recently broke my record. Cheeky! :(

Virginia Wolf

Some people say I'm one of the twentieth century's key writers, while others call me a snob. But I say, "Look at what big teeth I have!" So be careful what *you* call me!

Mary Cassette

I made *recorded* history. No, no, not as a singer. I know, the cassette threw you. As a woman artist, and in a time when women weren't accepted as having artistic talent, I proved them wrong!

Hippopotamus Bosch

Due to the Black Death, the chu
hired me to paint scary scene.
to show what happens when yc
lose faith. *Boo!*

Edgar A. Poet

I was a *raven* poet
who is perhaps nevermore.
But my dark and gloomy tales
shall live forevermore.
So despite all the fright, it has
served me right to *write!*

Susan Bee Anthony

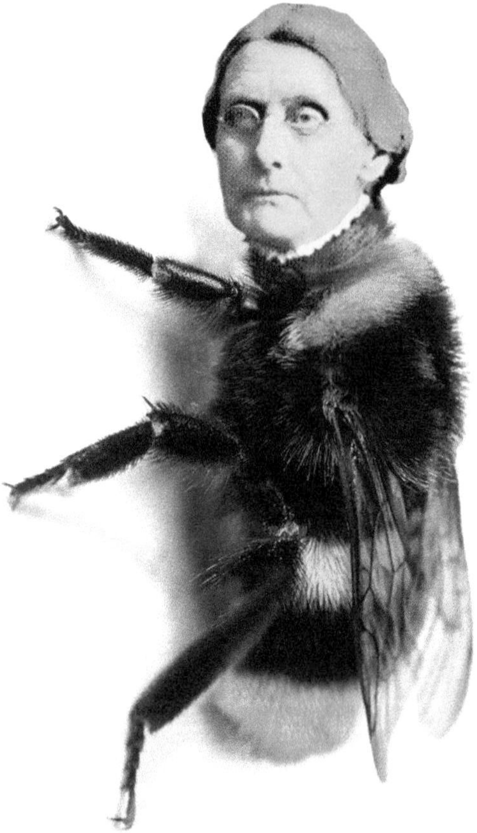

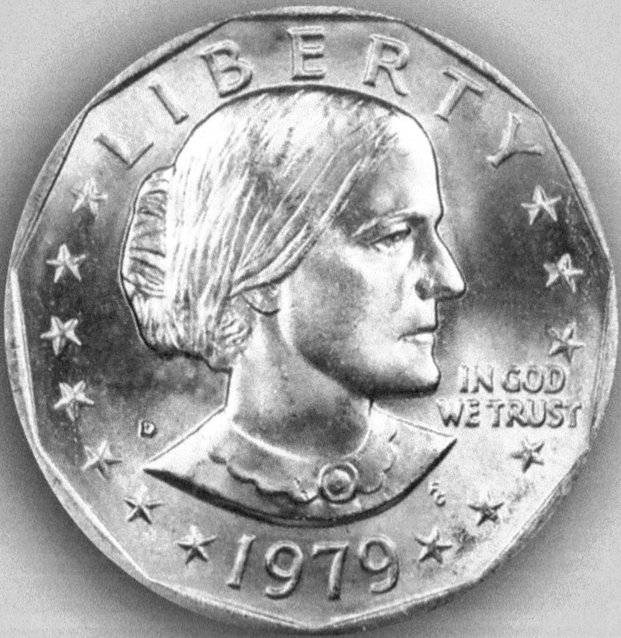
LIBERTY
IN GOD WE TRUST
D
1979

SALVADOR DOLLY

I painted surreal worlds of dreams, where anything is possible. I bet Ken can't do that!

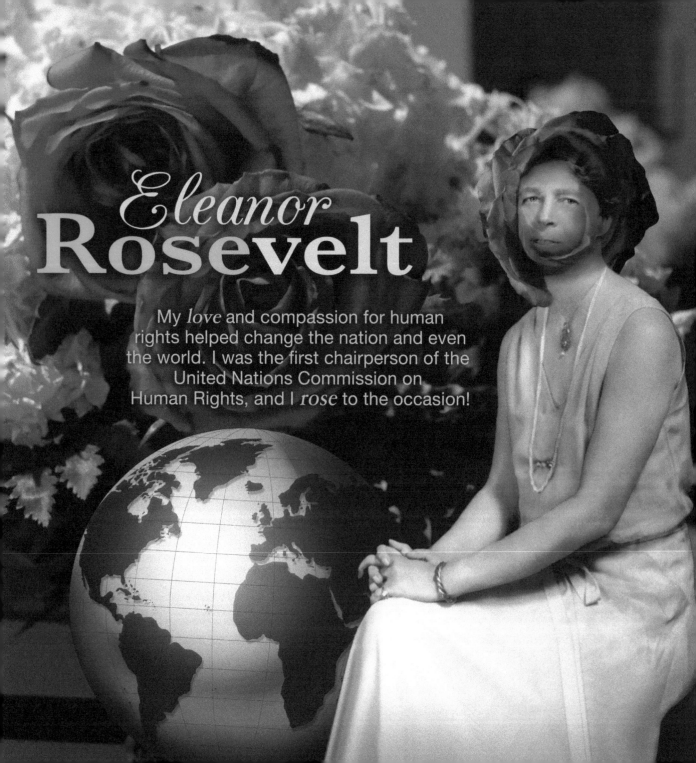

Eleanor
Rosevelt

My *love* and compassion for human rights helped change the nation and even the world. I was the first chairperson of the United Nations Commission on Human Rights, and I *rose* to the occasion!

MARTIN LUTHER KINGPIN Jr.

I was the kingpin of the civil rights movement that peacefully brought blacks and whites together. These pins look mighty fine, don't they? Especially that handsome devil up front!

MICHELANJELLO

Sculpture was my passion, and I could sculpt anything, be it out of a block of Carrara marble or tasty Jello!

As you can see, even my David likes to rub elbows with greatness!

AUGUSTUS

SUNDAY	MONDAY	TUESDAY	WEDNESDAY			URDAY
1	2	3	4			7
8		10	11			14
		17	18		20	21
	23	24				28
29	30	31				

As a teenager, I outsmarted Cicero, the ultimate intellect of my age, and Marc Antony, the leading general of my age, to rid Rome of their corrupt regime and begin the Roman Empire, which lasted over 500 years. Many have emulated aspects of my empire, including the young United States of America. Oh yes, purple is the color of royalty and the month of August was named in my honor. Pretty cool, huh?

Thomas Edisun

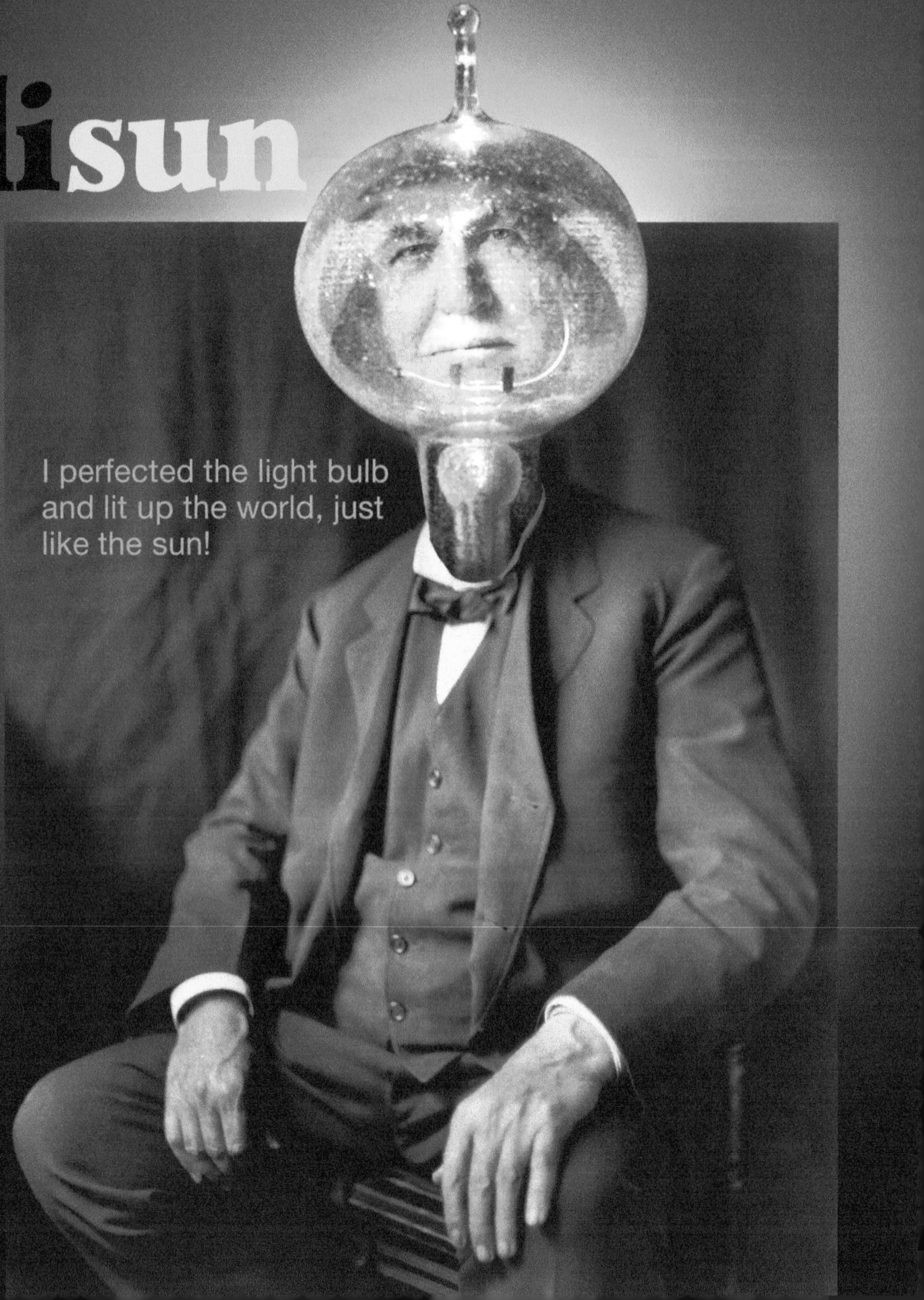
I perfected the light bulb
and lit up the world, just
like the sun!

Sergei Procoughiev

I compose great Russkie musik, but Stalin de tyrant try to crush my creativity.

But I cough in his face! Ya, cough! Real hard, like this, and compose, how do you say, killer musik! Nasty, sweet, cool stuff. You listen, you like, you try. Da?

Guglielmo
Macaroni

The only thing I love better than macaroni is wireless. All your Wi-Fi and cell phones are byproducts of wireless technology, which I invented back in the early 1900s. So every time you talk or text to your buddies, or play on your laptop with Wi-Fi, think of macaroni, I mean me! *Mangia!*

Madame Curious

I was a curious Polish-French scientist.
I won two Nobel Prizes, one for my research
with radiation, and the other for chemistry.
It pays to be curious!

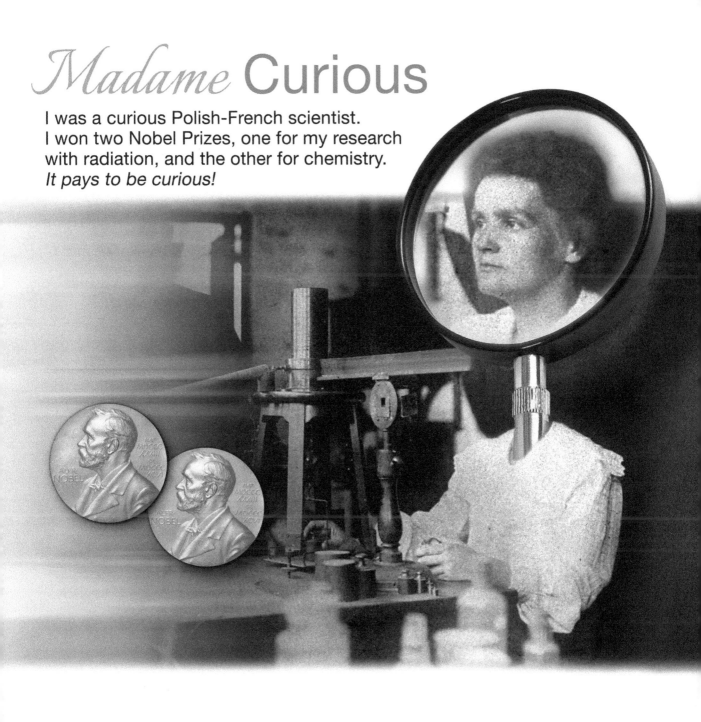

Queen Elizardbreath

I ruled England and Ireland for 44 years.

Yes, 44 bloody years!

And I even defeated the Spanish Armada.

So, yes, my long reign and success is simply *breath* taking!

Ronald **RAYGUN**

My Star Wars program zapped the Soviet Union's confidence, forcing them to finally back down. That's when I told Gorbachev to "tear down this wall" in Berlin, thus ending the Cold War and making America's future look mighty bright!

PABALO PICAXxO

I liked to see things Differently.
And that was no AXident!

Now it's **your** turn to think
differently and be creative.

And if anyone looks at you
as if you have two eyes on one
side of your head, say
"Picass-*GO away!*"
and continue your journey.
Good luck!

Actual Names

Mark Twain: November 30, 1835 – April 21, 1910

Leonardo Da Vinci: April 15, 1452 – May 2, 1519

Amelia Earhart: July 24, 1897 – Disappeared July 2, 1937

Giacomo Puccini: December 22, 1858 – November 29, 1924

Vincent van Gogh: March 30, 1853 – July 29, 1890

George Washington: February 22, 1732 – December 14, 1799

Albert Einstein: March 14, 1879 – April 18, 1955

Harriet Tubman: 1822 – March 10, 1913

Michelangelo Caravaggio: September 29, 1571 – July 18, 1610

Franz Liszt: October 22, 1811 – July 31, 1886

Queen Victoria: May 24, 1819 – January 22, 1901

Virginia Woolf: January 25, 1882 – March 28, 1941

Mary Cassatt: May 22, 1844 – June 14, 1926

Hieronymus Bosch: 1450 – August 9, 1516

Actual Names

Edgar Allan Poe: January 19, 1809 – October 7, 1849

Susan B. Anthony: February 15, 1820 – March 13, 1906

Salvador Dali: May 11, 1904 – January 23, 1989

Eleanor Roosevelt: October 11, 1884 – November 7, 1962

Martin Luther King Jr.: January 15, 1929 – April 4, 1968

Michelangelo Buonarroti: March 6, 1475 – February 18, 1564

Augustus Caesar: September 23, 63 BC – August 19, 14 AD

Thomas Edison: February 11, 1847 – October 18, 1931

Sergei Prokofiev: April 23, 1891 – March 5, 1953

Guglielmo Marconi: April 25, 1874 – July 20, 1937

Madame Curie: November 7, 1867 – July 4, 1934

Queen Elizabeth: September 7, 1533 – March 24, 1603

Ronald Reagan: February 6, 1911 – June 5, 2004

Pablo Picasso: October 25, 1881 – April 8, 1973